I Want
To Do
Yoga Too.

By Carole P. Roman

For Hallie,
who showed me with a little
faith, patience, and courage,
you can do anything.
You go, girl!

Mommy and Hallie went to

the yoga studio.

Mommy said, "You stay with Robin, while I go do yoga."

Hallie pouted and said, "I want to do yoga too, Mommy."

Robin took Hallie's hand and said, "We are going to have so much fun today!"

Hallie sniffed and repeated, "I really, *really* want to do yoga too."

"Well," Robin said, "let's pretend to be a tree. Trees are peaceful, quiet, and strong. Can you stand on one leg and put your hands in the air?"

Hallie stood very still. She copied Robin and rested her foot against her calf, making a triangle with her leg. She raised her hands in the air and said, "But I want to do yoga too!"

Robin said, "Now, put one leg behind you. Lift it up, and put your hands out like an airplane's wings."

Hallie did just that. Admiring herself in the mirror, she thought she looked like a sleek jet. Balancing on one leg, arms spread wide, she complained, "But I want to do yoga too."

Robin sat on the floor and put the soles of her feet together. She moved her knees in a waving motion. "Come be a butterfly with me."

Hallie sat down, and just like Robin, she flapped and flapped her knees. She looked just like a beautiful butterfly. Feeling light as a feather, she giggled.

"But I want to do yoga too!"

Next, Robin lay down on her stomach. She raised her head and chest off the floor. She whispered, "I am a cobra."

"Me too!" said Hallie, with a big smile. "This is so much fun!"

They both hissed together. "Hisssss."

"Oh my goodness," said Mommy. "Look at all these snakes!"

Hallie ran over to her mother. "Mommy, you left and I wanted to do yoga too."

"But you did do yoga, Hallie," Robin said. "First, we did Tree and then Airplane. We followed with Butterfly and finished with Cobra."

"Oh," Hallie said. "I just love yoga! Can we do yoga again?"

"Of course, Hallie," said Mommy. "Yoga is over for today, but we can come back tomorrow."

20096272R00014

Made in the USA
Charleston, SC
27 June 2013